WEASELS

For Mum, Dad, Chris
and everyone else.

First published in 2013 by Nosy Crow Ltd
The Crow's Nest, 10a Lant Street
London SE1 1QR
www.nosycrow.com

ISBN 978 0 85763 200 5 (PB)

Nosy Crow and associated logos are trademarks and /or registered trademarks
of Nosy Crow Ltd.

Text and illustration © Elys Dolan 2013
The right of Elys Dolan to be identified as the author
and illustrator of this work has been asserted.

A CIP catalogue record for this book is available
from the British Library.
Printed in Spain
3 5 7 9 8 6 4

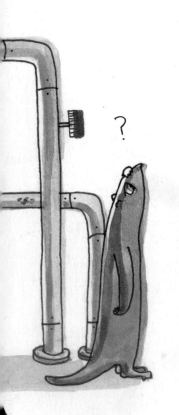

Weasels...

. . . what do you think they do all day?

Eat nuts and berries?

Frolic in the leaves?

Lurk in the dark?

Argue with squirrels?

Hide in their weasel holes?

Well, all of these are wrong.

What they really do is . . .

But something has gone very badly wrong.

Who turned the
lights out?

Was that supposed
to happen?

Why is there a wet
patch here?

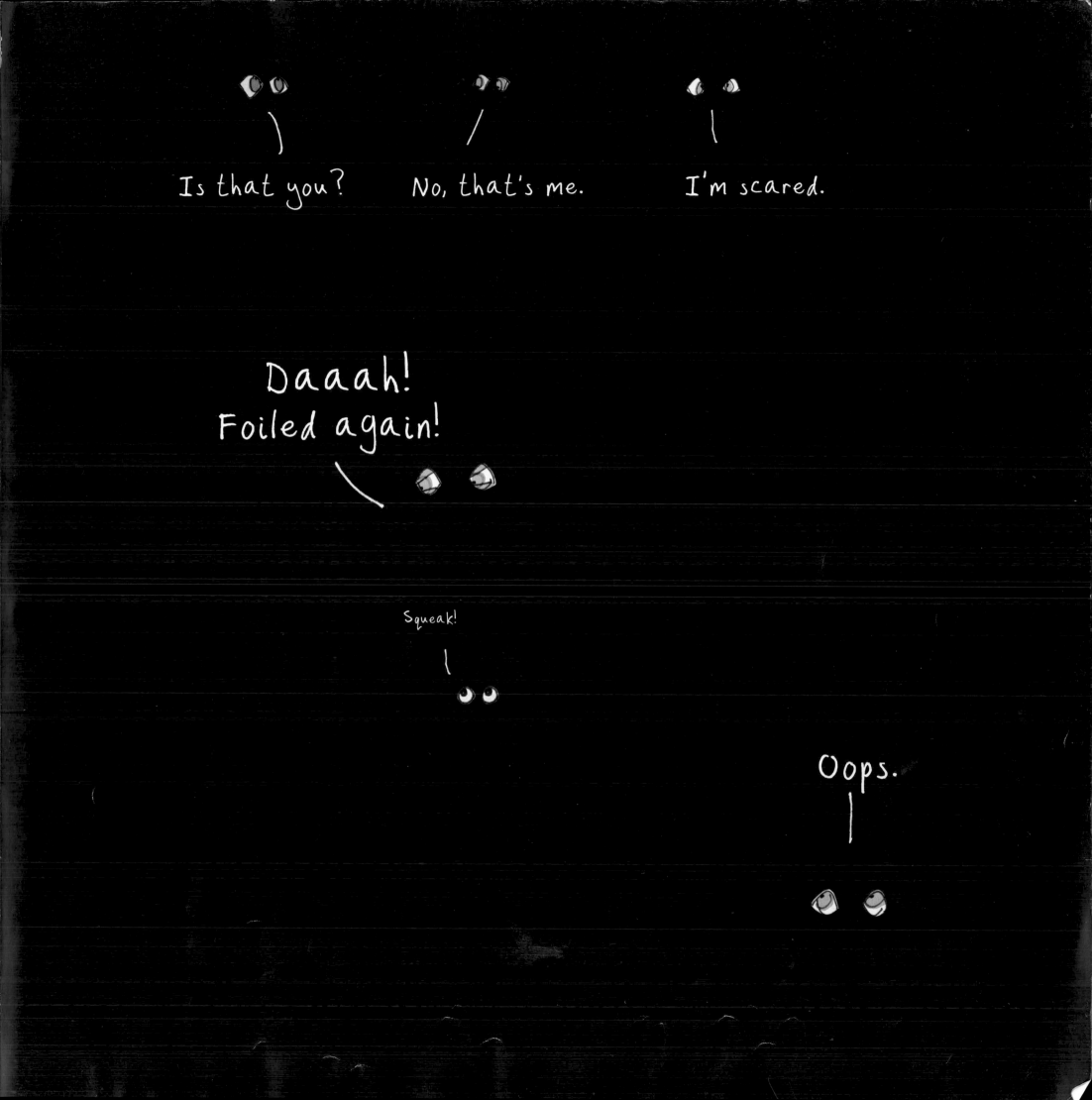

In the control room it seems that there are a few technical difficulties.

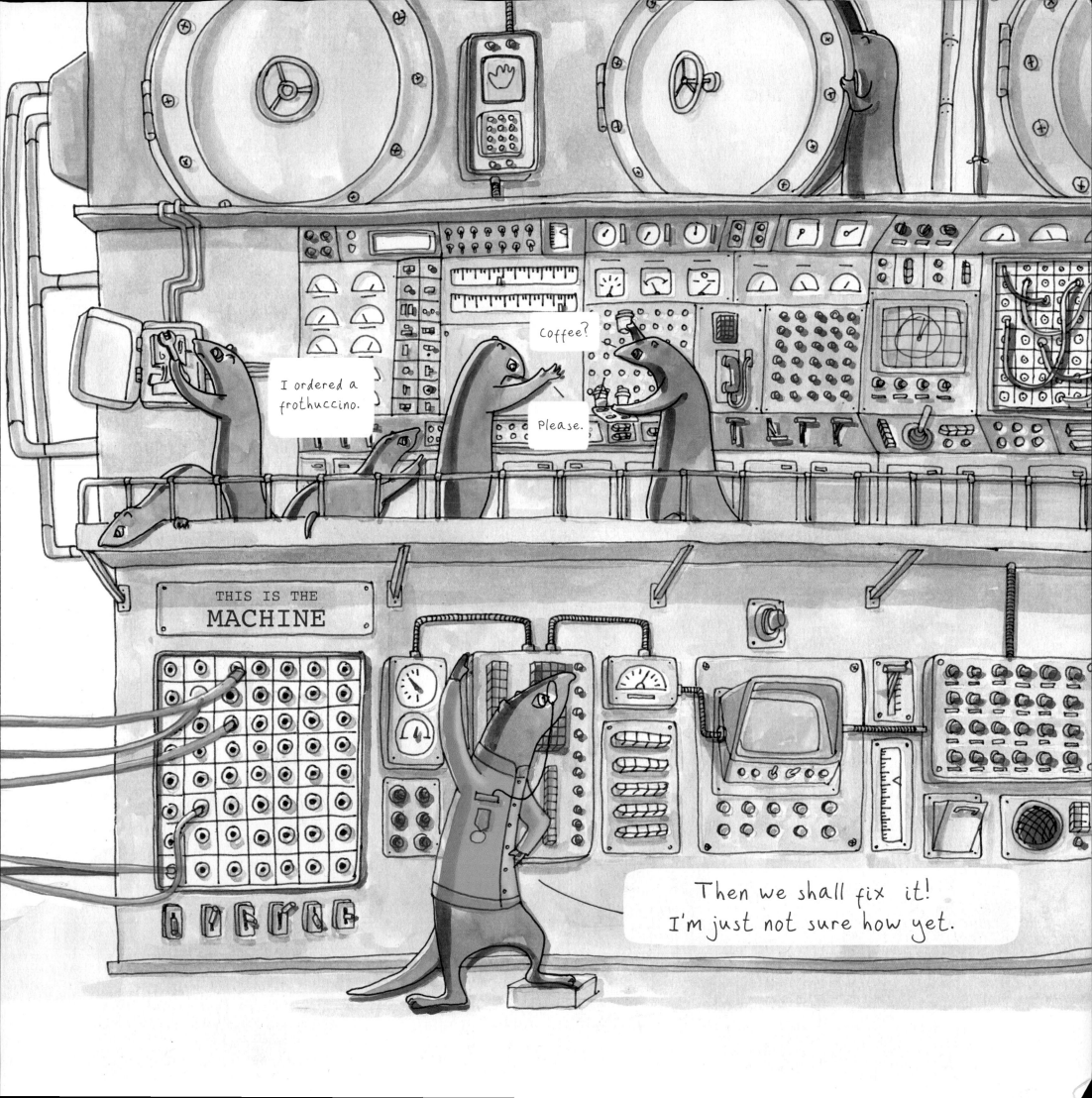

But technical difficulties won't stop a weasel . . .

...though they do like to stick to the rules.

Minister for DEMOLITION

Minister for HEALTH and SAFETY

BEST IN SHOW

Did you sleep through the whole thing?

Weaseltopia

ROGUE

THIS SEASON'S EYE PATCH

NEW

Much better.

DO NOT UNPLUG